STEPPING STONE STORIES

Linda Saves the Day
by Dr. Lawrence Balter

UNDERSTANDING FEAR

Illustrated by Roz Schanzer

BARRON'S

New York • London • Toronto • Sydney

All inquiries should be addressed to:
Barron's Educational Series, Inc.
250 Wireless Boulevard
Hauppauge, NY 11788

International Standard Book No. 0-8120-6117-9

Library of Congress Catalog No. 89-6604

Library of Congress Cataloging-in-Publication Data

Balter, Lawrence.
Linda saves the day.
Summary: Linda's mother patiently helps her overcome her
intense fear of dogs so that Linda is able to attend a party given by
a friend who owns a dog. Includes a discussion of phobias and how
to handle them.
[1. Fear—Fiction. 2. Dogs—Fiction] I. Schanzer, Rosalyn, ill. II.
Title. III. Series: Balter, Lawrence. Stepping stone stories.
PZ7.B2139Li   1989   [E]   89-6604
ISBN 0-8120-6117-9

PRINTED IN HONG KONG

9012   4900   987654321

Dear Parents and Teachers:

The books in this series were written to help young children better understand their own feelings and the feelings of others. It is hoped that by hearing these stories, or by reading them, children will see that they are not alone with their worries. They should also learn that there are constructive ways to deal with potentially disrupting circumstances.

All too often children's feelings are brushed aside by adults. Sometimes, because we want to protect youngsters and keep them happy, we inadvertently trivialize their concerns. But it is essential that we identify their emotions and understand their concerns before setting out to change things.

Children, of course, are more likely to act on their feelings rather than to reflect on them. After all, reflection requires tolerance which, in turn, calls for a degree of maturity. A first step, however, is learning to label and to talk about one's feelings.

I also hope to convey to parents and others who care for children that while some of a child's reactions may be troublesome, in all likelihood they are the normal by-products of some difficult situation with which the child is trying to cope. This is why children deserve our loving and patient guidance during their often painful and confusing journey toward adulthood.

Obviously, books can do only so much toward promoting self-understanding and problem-solving. I hope these stories will provide at least a helpful point of departure.

Lawrence Balter, Ph. D.

On a Friday afternoon not too terribly long ago in the town of Crescent Canyon a bunch of kids were getting ready to go to Alfred's birthday party.

"Are you dressed yet, Linda?" Mrs. Diaz called. There was no answer.

"Linda," she called again to her daughter.
Still no answer.
So Mrs. Diaz decided to check.

"What's the matter?" she asked.
"Why aren't you ready yet? You'll be
late for Alfred's party."
"I don't want to go," announced Linda.

"Why not?" Linda's mother asked with surprise.
"You'll have a good time. Alfred will be so
disappointed if you don't go."
"No!" Linda insisted.
She was not her usual, cheerful self.

"Come on," Mrs. Diaz coaxed. "I'll help you get dressed."

"No!"

"Don't you feel well? Does anything hurt?" her mother asked. "You don't seem to have a fever."

"I don't want to go to that house," Linda blurted out.

"My goodness, you're trembling. Did something happen to you there?" Mrs. Diaz asked.

"Nothing!" Linda answered.

Mrs. Diaz was puzzled.

"Well, if you won't tell me why you won't go, I can't help you," Mrs. Diaz said. "So you'd better get dressed. Alfred is expecting you."

"You can't make me!" Linda yelled.

"What's going on?" asked Linda's older sister, Lucy.

"No! Go away!" Linda shouted. "Get out of my room!"
"What's wrong with her, Mom?" Lucy asked.
"She doesn't want to go to Alfred's birthday party," Mrs. Diaz explained.
"Oh, can I go?" asked Lucy. "I want to see the new puppy."

Linda let out a great big howl and then she started to cry.
Lucy started barking and pretending to be a puppy.
The more she did it, the harder Linda cried.

WOOF!
WOOF!

"You're afraid of a puppy!" Lucy said.
"No, I'm not," sobbed Linda.
"Yes, you are. Yes, you are. You're a scaredy cat!"
teased Lucy.
"That's enough of that now," said Mrs. Diaz sternly
to Lucy.

"Are you afraid of the dog, Linda?" Mrs. Diaz asked.
Linda nodded sheepishly.
"But why?" her mother asked.
Linda thought very hard and then just shrugged.
"Is it because Danny's dog knocked you down that time?
Or did you have a bad dream about a dog? Or maybe it's
because Mrs. Bijou's dog has such a loud bark."
"No . . . maybe . . . I just don't know," Linda wailed.

"Baby, baby!" Lucy chanted. "Scaredy cat!"
"Now just quit the teasing," Mrs. Diaz said. "Tell me, what kind of dog did Alfred get?"
"It's just a puppy," Lucy answered.
"Come on, Linda. Let's go to see Alfred's puppy," Mrs. Diaz suggested. "It's probably so cute and small you'll see that there's nothing to be afraid of."

Linda began to tremble again.
She was about to cry.
"I have an idea," offered her mother. "I'll call
Alfred's mother and ask her to keep the dog in
another room. Okay?"
Linda calmed down a little.
"Lucy, bring us your book about dogs. I'll make that call
while you start to get ready," Mrs. Diaz said to Linda.
"It's okay," called Mrs. Diaz, just as Linda pulled on her
first sock. "Alfred's dad said he would keep the dog away.
Now let's take a quick look at Lucy's book."

They all looked.

"See, here's a dalmatian, the kind of dog the fire department has," Mrs. Diaz pointed out. "And here's a collie. They help farmers keep the sheep from wandering off. And here's a dog that helps a blind person. At bedtime tonight we'll read the rest of the book. Now it's time to go."

The sun was blazing hot on the way to Alfred's,
but Linda's hands were cold and clammy.
Mrs. Diaz detoured past the pet store.
They stopped to look in the window.
The puppies were frisky and playful as Linda
watched cautiously.
"Sometimes we don't know why we are afraid of
things. But there are some ways to help us stop
being scared," her mother said.
Linda still felt jittery.

"Now think about eating a slice of birthday cake," Mrs. Diaz said softly while they watched the dogs. "And think about the party and the games."
Linda began to feel a little better.
But she still clutched her mother's hand tightly.

"Let's pretend that you're a dog and I'm taking you for a walk to Alfred's," suggested Mrs. Diaz. "Now, you're supposed to growl."
Linda made a noise that sounded more like a squeak than a growl.
"How about a really loud bark?" asked Mrs. Diaz.
Linda's bark sounded more like a cough.
Mrs. Diaz laughed.
Linda smiled.
"Listen to this one," her mother said. "BRAACH RUFF!" she barked, and they both laughed.

SQUEAK!

"I know another game," Mrs. Diaz said as they came closer to Alfred's house. "Pretend you're in a big room and there are a lot of dogs and they're all barking at once. It sounds like a lot of yelling and screaming."

Linda started to feel scared.
Her heart jumped in her chest and her legs felt tired.

"Remember, this is just make-believe," Mrs. Diaz reminded. "It's to help you to not be so afraid."

"There is another part to the game," her mother said.
"There's a secret trick. You're wearing a special dinosaur
coat. All the ferocious make-believe dogs are around
you but they can't hurt you. Come on, try it."
Linda stopped walking and closed her eyes.
In her mind she saw what her mother said.

When she thought about their teeth and all the
barking, she did not like it.
But then she made herself think about the
tough dinosaur coat with all the spikes on her
dinosaur back and tail.
That made her feel better.
They started walking again.

By the time they arrived at Alfred's, the other children
were already there.
Linda let go of her mother's hand but felt a little afraid.
She looked around and there was no puppy in sight.
So she joined her friends in some games.

After a few rounds of musical chairs, Linda volunteered
to run out to the backyard to get some clothespins
so they could play drop the clothespins in the bottle.
She had good aim and knew that she would be a winner.
She ran through the kitchen and out onto the porch.
Then she crossed the yard toward the clothesline.

Suddenly Alfred's puppy scampered down the
steps and rolled onto the lawn.
Somebody must have left a door open.
He saw Linda and started to run playfully toward her.
Her heart fluttered.
Nobody else was there with her.
She wanted to get away so badly, but her legs
would not move her from the spot.
He kept coming.

All at once the puppy turned away from Linda
and darted toward the bushes near the street.
Linda caught her breath.
This was her chance to get into the house safely.
Then she saw that the puppy was scrambling
through the bushes.
Cars were whizzing by the house.
Another few steps and the puppy would be in
the dangerous street.
Linda heard a big truck approaching.
"Puppy, puppy!" she yelled as loudly as she could.
The small dog backed out of the bushes and flipped over.
"Wait, puppy!" Linda shouted as she ran.

She scooped the dusty puppy into her arms just
as the big truck went rumbling by.
"Foolish little puppy!" she scolded. "I've got you.
You're safe now."
Alfred's puppy just licked her nose.
It felt yucky and wet, but nice, too.

Even though it was Alfred's birthday
everyone made a big fuss over Linda.
"That was very brave," said her mother.
"Thank you for saving my puppy,"
said Alfred.
"Thanks for coming to Alfred's party," said
Mrs. Andrews.
Linda felt happy.

That night after her bath, Linda's father told her
he was proud of her.
"You really saved the day," he said.
"No, I saved the puppy," Linda joked.
Instead of her usual bedtime story, Mrs. Diaz
read to Linda from Lucy's book about dogs.
Even though lots of dogs do good things, Linda
knew enough not to touch strange dogs.
And even though she liked Alfred's puppy, she
would probably still cross the street whenever
she saw Mrs. Bijou's big old barking dog.
But now she knew that she didn't have to be
afraid of *all* dogs.
And she knew that there were things she could
do when she felt scared.

When she finished reading, her mother tucked her in.
"You certainly had a big day," her mother said.
"Good night, and sweet dreams."
"No!" Linda said loudly. "I'm too scared! There's a dog
in my bed!" she said, trying not to laugh.
"Oh no, not again," said Mrs. Diaz with a smile.
Linda grabbed her old stuffed poodle at the foot
of her bed and hugged him. They both had a big
laugh together.

It was going to be a night of lovely dreams of
dinosaurs, puppy dogs, and birthday cake for
Linda, the kid who saved the day that afternoon
in Crescent Canyon.

About This Book

This story is about a child who develops an irrational fear, or phobia. Phobias are fairly common and are usually short-lived in young children.

We all have fears. Without them, we might not exercise prudence and caution when we should. So fears, as such, are not bad for us. It is when they are unduly inhibiting or when they do little to protect us from real hazards, that they become problems.

In young children, the most common phobias are fears of the dark, loud noises, and being lost. Some children develop fears of small bugs, monsters, and hidden lions and tigers. Other are intensely afraid of clowns and loud singing in nursery school.

Some phobias are easier to understand than others. If a child were stung by a bee or knocked down by a large dog, we could readily see the possible origin of an exaggerated fear of all bugs or domestic animals. In the absence of such evidence, however, we may feel at a loss to understand the basis for such irrational behavior.

There is a view that suggests the child's feelings are at the bottom of the problem. Feelings of anger and rage, which are present in every child, are particularly difficult for the phobic child to acknowledge. Unwittingly, the child disguises and disowns these feelings. They are externalized and given a form. In this way, violent emotions can masquerade as ferocious animals or monsters. So, while these inner feelings appear to be under control, they still cause fear but are now perceived as coming from the outside.

You may become impatient with a phobic child because of the inconveniences that are bound to crop up or because you can't tolerate irrational behavior. However, you must never humiliate a child or use force to get a child to overcome a phobia. To be tossed into a swimming pool, for example, is no way to help a child conquer a fear of the water. Rather, patience and empathy should be the basic ingredients.

Several techniques are useful in encouraging a child to overcome a phobia. One is to help the child acknowledge feelings of frustration, dissatisfaction, and anger. A phobic child must learn that violent feelings and fantasies do not lead to uncontrollable destruction or rejection. In other words, although actions must be controlled, thoughts are free to roam.

Another approach is to reduce the child's dread systematically through a series of steps designed to increase the child's tolerance for the frightening thing. In gradual increments, the child is encouraged to overcome the loathing by using relaxation techniques, creative imagination, and courage.

In this story, Mrs. Diaz helps her daughter, Linda, cope with her fear of dogs. It is about one fear only and presents only a few techniques for dealing with it. While I could not possibly cover a representative array of fears or the numerous ways to deal with them, I hope this story will provide a basis from which to build your own strategies should the occasion arise. Naturally, it is important to realize that there are times when fears and phobias require professional help.